The Hedgehog Feast

First published in Great Britain by Michael Joseph Ltd,
52 Bedford Square, London WC1B 3EF, in association with
Webb & Bower Ltd, 21 Southernhay West, Exeter, Devon EX1 1PR

June 1978
Second Impression November 1978

Copyright © Webb & Bower Ltd 1978

Drawings from *Animals Around Us* by Edith Holden and Martin Merrythought

Printed and bound in England by
W. S. Cowell Limited

The Hedgehog Feast is based on my great aunt Edith's water-colour
illustrations which were painted after 1911. It is unclear why all the
initials on the illustrations do not tally exactly with those of Edith Blackwell
Smith (née Holden) but following her marriage to Alfred Ernest Smith it is
known that she experimented with various monograms. My family inherited
these illustrations at the same time and together with her Nature Notes for
1906, recently published as *The Country Diary of an Edwardian Lady*.
Comparison with details in that book and her other work published at that
time proves beyond all reasonable doubt that the illustrations for *The
Hedgehog Feast* were the original work of my great aunt Edith Holden.

Rowena Stott

The Hedgehog Feast

by Edith Holden

Words by Rowena Stott

Michael Joseph/Webb & Bower

In the corner of a large orchard lived Hugh and Hilda Hedgehog with their three children, Holly, Henry and Hazel. Their house was tucked away in the undergrowth and lined with dry leaves to keep it warm.

One evening when Holly, Henry and Hazel were fast asleep in their bed, Hugh and Hilda sat by the fire. The evenings were drawing in and the leaves were beginning to fall. The next day they were giving a grand hibernation party and all the arrangements had to be made. There were invitations to write and deliver and, of course, they had to decide what food they were going to have.

Everyone was very excited and early next morning Hugh went out to collect some apples. On his way he tried to catch a snail for his breakfast. The apples had fallen off the trees and gleamed red and shiny in the green grass. "Now, how am I going to get these home?" said Hugh to himself. They were too big for him to carry in his arms. He sat down to think. Then he had a good idea.

F.S

"If I roll myself up into a ball I can stick the apples on my spines." And that is what he did. He looked very funny as he set off home.

Reuben Rat, out for a walk, was very startled to see some shining apples bobbing down the path, but he couldn't see Hugh underneath them. Hugh was a little frightened that Reuben might attack him, but he kept walking on, determined to get the apples home for the party.

From the other side of the path, William Weasel was craftily watching and waiting. All at once Reuben and William leapt towards the bobbing apples. They bounced into each other and rolled around in the dust. Hugh ran away as fast as he could, the apples rumbling after him. He left William Weasel and Reuben Rat scuffling furiously together.

Holly, Henry and Hazel had been looking out for their father, and when they saw him come running they went out to help him bring the rolling apples into the kitchen. Hilda was very pleased and said she would make a lovely spicy apple pie. Mouse the Maid who was helping squeaked, "It would be nice to have some cider too." So everyone agreed she should go and find some.

Hilda made some pastry and peeled and chopped up all the apples, singing happily to herself. But Holly, Henry and Hazel were beginning to get bored. Their mother wouldn't let them play with the pastry or eat the apples because she needed them. "Why don't you go and see if you can find something else to eat", she said. The little hedge-hogs jumped up and ran off towards the big farmhouse on the other side of the orchard.

They were very puffed when they got there, then, wondering what was inside, they decided to climb through a little open window. They had to help each other up, which was very uncomfortable. "Ow!" said Holly as she stepped on Henry's back, "You're prickling me. Ooh! Ouch!" The best way was to climb very quickly, but Holly went just a bit too fast.

Splash! She fell into a bowl of cream standing on the window-sill. The others laughed and laughed until she managed to clamber out. They had to lick the cream off her spines. Mmmmmmmmmm, delicious. They looked around the little room, but there was nothing else to eat so they climbed out of the window and set off back home.

They hadn't gone far before they came across a hoard of hazelnuts in the hollow of a tree. Hazel said, "Let's take some of these home for the party." Suddenly Henry looked up and gasped. It was Sandy Squirrel staring crossly down at them.

"What do you think you're doing", he said
sternly. "That's my winter hoard of nuts." The
little hedgehogs were so startled that they
scampered off before Sandy could say anything
else. He was an old family friend and hadn't
meant to frighten them. He decided to take some
of his special hoard to the party.

The hedgehog house was buzzing with excitement. Soon the guests started to arrive. Sandy Squirrel and Mouse the Maid's sister were first, followed by all the other animals who lived nearby: the Rabbit family, the Shrew family, Lizard, Frog and Beetle. And what a feast it was with so many delicious things to eat! Crispy salad, stuffed snails, gooseberry fool, damson cheese, bramble jelly, nuts, blackberries, and lots of cider to drink. But best of all was Hilda's lovely apple pie. Henry, Holly and Hazel were the first to go to bed. Everyone went on eating until they could eat no more and they all began to feel very, very sleepy indeed. And soon they were all ready for their long winter's sleep.

Facts about the Hedgehog

HEDGEHOG   Erinaceus Europaeus

A grey-brown animal which has yellow-tipped spines on its back and sides and coarse hair on its head and underside. The spines are not as sharp as the porcupine's, and a human can pick up a hedgehog comfortably. The legs and tail are very short in relation to the body; the eyes and ears small. Adult males are about 9 inches (229 millimetres) long.

The hedgehog is a native of Europe and lives in fields, open woods (but not dense ones), hedgerows and gardens throughout Britain. It lies hidden by day and comes out at night to hunt for food, which it finds through its keen senses of smell and hearing. It is most active at dusk and dawn. It feeds mainly on insects and their larvae, snails, slugs, worms and fallen fruit. There have been several accounts by reliable witnesses of hedgehogs gathering fruit and then impaling them for purposes of transport. The story has in fact existed since Pliny first mentioned it.

Hedgehogs mate between March and July. One or two litters of between three and seven young are born in nests of grass or leaves from May to September. A nest may be built in a hedge, under a tree root or in a disused rabbit hole. The mother suckles the young for a month, after which they start hunting for food.

Hedgehogs hibernate between October and early April in nests bigger than those in which they nurse their young and spend their summer days. They use leaves and pieces of moss to keep the rain out and to maintain an even temperature inside. They usually live for several years and one has been recorded as surviving in captivity until it was seventeen.

Their natural enemies are foxes and badgers.